TALENTS AND ABILITIES

RECOGNIZING STRENGTHS

DAVID MACHAJEWSKI

PowerKiDS press™

NEW YORK

Published in 2020 by The Rosen Publishing Group, Inc.
29 East 21st Street, New York, NY 10010

Editor: Rachel Gintner
Designer: Michael Flynn

Photo Credits: Cover AnaWhite/Shutterstock.com; cover, pp. 1, 3, 4, 6, 8, 10, 12–14, 16, 18–20, 22–24 (background) TairA/Shutterstock.com; p. 5 Fuse/Corbis/Getty Images; p. 7 Hill Street Studios/Blend Images/Getty Images; p. 9 AVAVA/Shutterstock.com; p. 11 Peathegee Inc/Blend Images/Getty Images; p. 12 Leonard Zhukovsky/Shutterstock.com; p. 13 MichaelJayBerlin/Shutterstock.com; p. 15 ImageFlow/Shutterstock.com; p. 16 Digital Media Pro/Shutterstock.com; p. 17 https://en.wikipedia.org/wiki/Wolfgang_Amadeus_Mozart#/media/File:Wolfgang-amadeus-mozart_1.jpg; p. 18 Chris Ware/Hulton Archive/Getty Images; p. 19 Christian Jung/Shutterstock.com; p. 21 Mischa Keijser/Cultura/Getty Images; p. 22 YAKOBCHUK VIACHESLAV/Shutterstock.com.

Cataloging-in-Publication Data

Names: Machajewski, David.
Title: Talents and abilities: recognizing strengths / David Machajewski.
Description: New York : PowerKids Press, 2020. | Series: Spotlight on social and emotional learning | Includes glossary and index.
Identifiers: ISBN 9781725302099 (pbk.) | ISBN 9781725302280 (library bound) | ISBN 9781725302198 (6pack)
Subjects: LCSH: Self-realization--Juvenile literature. | Self-actualization (Psychology) in adolescence--Juvenile literature. | Self-esteem--Juvenile literature. | Identity (Psychology)--Juvenile literature.
Classification: LCC BF637.S4 M33 2020 | DDC 158.1--dc23

Manufactured in the United States of America

CPSIA Compliance Information: Batch #CSPK19. For further information contact Rosen Publishing, New York, New York at 1-800-237-9932.

CONTENTS

CHAPTER ONE

YOU'VE GOT TALENT!

Have you ever heard someone ask the question, "What gets you out of bed in the morning?" People use this phrase, or saying, to find out what inspires others to do their best every day. The way a person answers this question may tell you something about their talents and strengths—the special qualities that can contribute to someone's **personality** and help them place their mark on the world.

Every person, no matter how young or old, has **unique** talents and strengths. These features often make us feel proud, happy, or satisfied to be who we are.

If your unique talents and strengths aren't clear to you right now, there's no need to worry. Finding and **appreciating** your talents takes time and patience. Approaching these qualities with curiosity is a good way to begin. So let's get started!

It's fun to greet the day with your talents and strengths in mind!

CHAPTER TWO

MANY WAYS TO BE TALENTED

During talent shows, performers bravely show off their talents in front of others. Some tell jokes while others play music. You might see dances, magic tricks, science experiments, or other unique performances.

Talent shows teach an important lesson—there's no "right" way to be talented. Although some talent shows are contests, talents can be valuable just by offering enjoyment to yourself and others.

For example, talents can help you decide which hobbies you like. Having hobbies can build **self-confidence** and can also help you make friends with like-minded people. Talents also can help you give back to others. If you have a talent for gardening, for instance, you might offer to help your neighbors with their yard work. In this case, you would be helping people while **honing** your talent—a win-win situation!

Ask your friends or family members if they've ever been to a talent show. You might be surprised to learn about the unique performances they've seen!

CHAPTER THREE

YOUR SPECIAL TALENTS

Let's talk about your talents. Identifying your own talents can feel **intimidating**, especially if you've never thought about them before. But you have plenty of time to try different things on for size. While certain skills come easier to some people compared to others, remember that your talents can be built up over time.

One way to identify your talents is to think about your **passions**. Being passionate about something means that you love or care about doing it. Your passions are like constant companions—they're specific things that keep your mind and body interested.

If you're unsure of your talents, ask yourself, "How do I like to spend my time?" or "Are there certain activities I love to do more than anything else?" The answers to these questions will help you identify your passions and, often, your talents.

We use mirrors to look at our outside appearance. Our passions and talents aren't often as easily seen as our appearance, but they still form a big part of who we are.

CHAPTER FOUR

UNDERSTANDING YOUR STRENGTHS

Your strengths are a mixture of knowledge and skills that help you succeed. They're the building blocks that help make up who you are.

1. **Recognize excitement.** Choose your goal. Make sure it's something you want to do. That will help you stay interested.

2. **Try new things.** You have lots of strengths that are waiting to be found. Trying new things helps uncover these unknown strengths.

3. **Notice what comes naturally.** If a certain activity is **intuitive** for you but challenging for others, that means you have natural strength in that area.

4. **Ask loved ones.** If you're still stumped, ask your friends or family about the strengths they see in you. Learning the opinions of others will provide new information about your strengths.

Friends are a great source of inspiration when you're learning about your strengths and talents.

CHAPTER FIVE

WEAKNESSES: PART OF US ALL

When something feels challenging, it can cause feelings of discomfort and even anger. When you struggle, remember that you're not alone. Just as every person has strengths, we all also have weaknesses. Weaknesses are the opposite of strengths, which means they can make certain activities feel challenging.

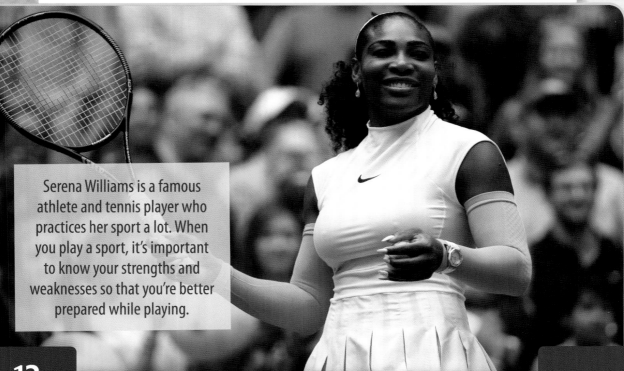

Serena Williams is a famous athlete and tennis player who practices her sport a lot. When you play a sport, it's important to know your strengths and weaknesses so that you're better prepared while playing.

You can understand yourself better when you
know your strengths and weaknesses.

STRENGTH | WEAKNESS

Having weaknesses doesn't mean that you should give up on a task or hobby. It just means that some tasks might require more effort than others.

For example, you might have played sports that are hard for you to do. But that doesn't mean you can't have fun! You can always ask your coaches or fellow players for tips on how to improve your skills or you can try to find another position that might be a better fit. Just like you can build your talents, you can practice to overcome or rise above your weaknesses.

CHAPTER SIX

WHERE DO TALENTS COME FROM?

You might be wondering where talents come from. The answer is a bit tricky, but to help understand it, consider your own experiences.

Have you ever tried something for the first time and found it easy and fun, while others found it challenging? Scientific **research** suggests that some people are born with **innate** talents. This means, in part, that their genetic makeup provides them with a special ability to complete certain tasks with ease. If you're especially skilled at activities such as chess, math, music, or sports, your genes might play a part in those talents.

Very rarely, an individual can be described as a **prodigy** in a specific area. But for most people, saying all skills are the product of genes only tells one part of the story about talents.

Each cell in the human body has thousands of genes. Genes carry information that impacts your traits, which are features that your parents pass on to you.

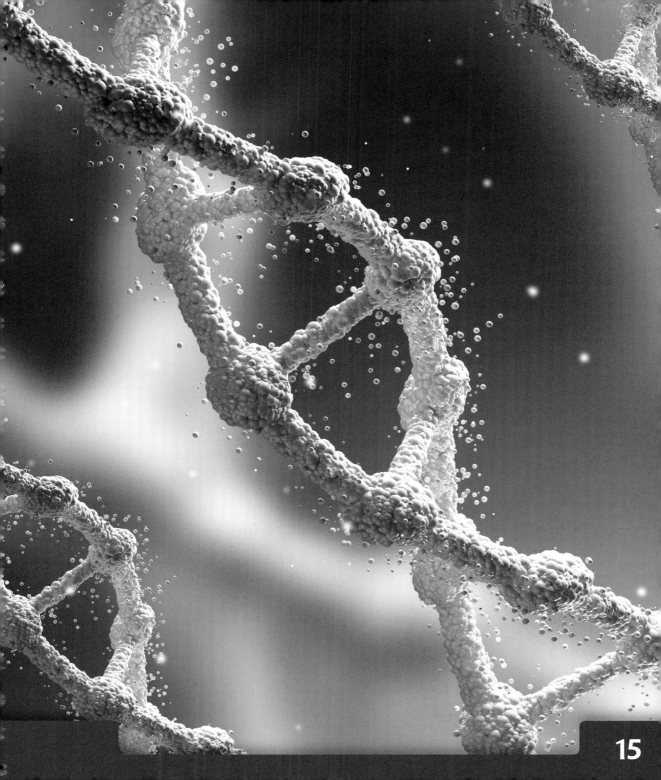

CHAPTER SEVEN

THE ART OF PRACTICE

It isn't just genes that make you talented. As cool as it might be to wake up one day and play guitar like a rock star or to speak a new language, mastering skills takes a lot of practice. In fact, one author who writes books about talent suggests that mastering a skill requires at least 10,000 hours of practice!

Practice can be challenging, but there are many ways to improve. If you want to master ballet, for example, you might think the only way to practice is by putting in long hours at a studio. While time spent taking lessons and dancing is very important, you can also grow as a performer by attending performances, watching videos on the Internet, or reading books about the art form. Often, learning about these activities helps inspire us to keep practicing.

Wolfgang Amadeus Mozart, a famous composer and musician, began composing music at age five. Mozart is remembered as a prodigy, but he also practiced every day.

CHAPTER EIGHT

MAKING MISTAKES

There are many ways to describe mistakes. Common words used are "setbacks," "errors," or "bloopers." Perhaps there are so many words to describe mistakes because they're so common. Everyone makes mistakes. Whether they're big or small, mistakes are a normal part of life.

When you're practicing, mistakes are bound to happen. Sometimes, it seems like giving up is the best choice, especially if you keep making mistakes. But mistakes are actually part of your journey as you grow your strengths and talents.

Alexander Fleming, shown here, accidentally discovered the antibiotic penicillin in 1928. Penicillin has made the world a safer, healthier place to live.

Chocolate chip cookies, penicillin, and microwave ovens were all created by mistake. Who knows—your next mistake might turn out to be an amazing invention!

Mistakes offer opportunities to learn and grow. They can provide ideas about how to do something differently, giving us information on what is or isn't working when we're reaching for new goals. So the next time you make a mistake, consider it a learning moment, not a failure. With this mindset, you'll be back on track in no time!

CHAPTER NINE

APPRECIATING OTHERS

Talents can be shared far and wide. They can be used to help others, like when a good cook brings a sick neighbor some delicious soup. Talents can also be used to entertain, such as when a musician shares their talents with the world by posting a performance video online or playing a concert. Our talents can help others grow, such as when a gifted math student helps struggling classmates with their homework. The possibilities of talents are endless!

The next time you see a loved one use their talent for the benefit of others, make sure you show your appreciation. You can give them a high five, write them a note, or send them a thoughtful gift. These are just a few ideas on how to express **gratitude**, which helps **cultivate** friendships and show people that you care about them.

Talents bring people together. Showing gratitude for others is a great way to be a friend.

CHAPTER TEN

FIND YOUR TALENT!

Recognizing talents takes time and patience. You should be better prepared to discover your special talents after reading this book! Taking the time to recognize your natural passions, strengths, and even weaknesses will help you know yourself better as a person. There's no person quite like you, so the talents you share with the world will be unique and valuable.

Remember, if you struggle to understand your talents or strengths, you're not alone. Knowing and developing talents takes time. You can always ask your friends, family, and teachers for insight into what makes you special. Your community can also help cheer you on as you practice your skills. Even if you make mistakes (we all do!), regular practice and exploration will give you the knowledge you need to make the world a better place with your unique talents.

GLOSSARY

appreciate (uh-PREE-shee-ayt) To understand something's worth or value.

cultivate (CUHL-tuh-vayt) To grow and care for something.

gratitude (GRAH-tuh-tood) The state of being grateful.

hone (HOHN) To practice something, such as a skill or strength, to get better at that activity.

innate (ih-NAYT) A quality belonging to someone from birth.

intimidating (in-TIH-muh-day-ting) Causing feelings of fear, uncertainty, or anxiety.

intuitive (ihn-TOO-uh-tiv) Understood quickly, such as when an activity feels easy to do or an idea is easily learned.

passion (PAA-shun) A powerful feeling of desire or longing.

personality (puhr-suh-NAA-luh-tee) The set of qualities and ways of behaving that make a person different from other people.

prodigy (PRAH-duh-jee) A young person who is unusually talented in some way.

research (REE-surch) Careful study to find new knowledge.

self-confidence (SELF–CAHN-fuh-duhns) Being sure of oneself and enjoying one's own powers and abilities.

unique (yoo-NEEK) Special or different from anything else.

INDEX

PRIMARY SOURCE LIST

Page 12
Serena Williams. Photograph. Leonard Zhukovsky. September 3, 2016. Billie Jean King National Tennis Center in New York.

Page 17
Wolfgang Amadeus Mozart. Oil painting. Barbara Krafft. 1819. Gesellschaft der Musikfreunde.

Page 18
Sir Alexander Flemming (1881–1955). Photograph. Chris Ware. January 1, 1954. Hulton Archive.

WEBSITES

Due to the changing nature of Internet links, PowerKids Press has developed an online list of websites related to the subject of this book. This site is updated regularly. Please use this link to access the list: www.powerkidslinks.com/SSEL/talents